Also by Wolf Erlbruch

Duck, Death and the Tulip (Gecko Press, 2008)

Wolf Erlbruch is a German illustrator and writer of more than
25 picture books for children, among them Werner Holzwarth's
The Story of the Little Mole Who Knew it was None of His Business
and *Duck, Death and the Tulip.* He won the Hans Christian
Andersen Award in 2006 for his continued contribution to
children's literature.

WOLF ERLBRUCH
THE FEARSOME FIVE

GECKO PRESS

Horrible. Toad's yellow eyes looked even more sickly in the moonlight. And the warts didn't help: fat warts, all over his face. Awful.

'Yes, well,' — sharp as a knife, Rat's voice was a stab in the dark — 'none of us is getting any prettier.'

'Go easy on him, Garbage Gobbler.' Bat was hanging out after the night's flying. 'Toad's heart is weak.'

Rat scowled at Bat. 'You're no picture yourself, Umbrella Boy. Who did you scare tonight?'

'**M**e! He scared me.' Spider dropped from the bridge overhead.

'You? You needed a good shock, you leggy old spinster!' Bat whacked at her web with a wingtip. Spider whizzed back up in a huff.

'**H**ush, everyone! Listen,' Bat hissed. He had excellent hearing. Rat and Spider froze.

'*Now* what?' Toad was preoccupied, weighed down with self-pity. But now he too heard it, too: a curious chuckling, coming their way.

'Someone's laughing.' Rat was sure.

'Probably at us,' muttered Toad.

'What's this gloomy gang?' they heard the stranger cackle as he approached out of the darkness. 'Looks like the cry-baby club.'

'Hyena,' Rat whispered. He had been to Africa and knew about such things.

'Hideous,' said Toad, too loudly, 'and laughing doesn't help matters.'

Hearing that, Hyena composed himself and said in a voice that was almost motherly, 'I'm sorry, my dears. Is there a problem?'

'Look at us!' Rat blurted. 'It's generally agreed that we're revolting. You find that funny?'

For a moment Hyena looked uncertain. Then he sat down. 'It doesn't matter a jot if others think you're ugly,' he said warmly. 'It's what you do that matters. I advise you to do something — anything.'

So saying, he took a gleaming instrument from his pocket and began to play it.

'Saxophone,' whispered Rat, who had been to New Orleans.

They listened, and found themselves carried away by the tune.

When it was over, Spider swooned. 'That's magical music.'

'Rather dreamy, isn't it?' Hyena peered through his green spectacles at them. 'And I'll bet you've forgotten how ugly I am.'

Rat saw exactly what he meant. As Hyena played his beautiful music, he had grown more and more appealing.

With a tiny smile, Rat took a ukulele from his own deep coat pocket and started to pick out a song.

It had been quiet overhead but now with the first light of dawn a delicate voice trickled down from the bridge. Spider was singing. Bat was so moved he almost lost his grip, but he pursed his lips and began to whistle a soulful accompaniment.

Toad couldn't sing or play, nor could he hold back any longer. 'I can make pancakes!' he cried, and his whole green face turned red.

There was a dumbfounded silence.

'You can make pancakes?' said Rat. 'Why on earth didn't you say so before?'

Hyena slapped his thigh in delight. Then he said quietly, 'I dare say it's no coincidence that four musicians and a pancake-maker have met under a bridge tonight.'

The other four looked at him expectantly, but he merely added, 'I wonder what happens next.'

It was Rat who suddenly twigged. 'I know! We can set up a kind of musical pancake place.'

'Exactly so.' Hyena smiled at the others.

Spider bounced with delight, and Bat sprang for joy, even though it was seven in the morning and time for bed. 'It's perfect!' he said. 'Everywhere you look there are pizza parlours, sausage stands and burger bars. But a pancake palace with music and dancing — now that's original.'

'Excellent,' said Hyena. 'All we need is the right spot.'

'But we have it already!' said Toad. 'It's pretty nice here under the bridge.' And it was true: in the rosy glow of early morning, the place held a certain charm.

To be sure, a few things were missing. There were no tables or chairs, and they'd have to fix the lighting — the moon didn't shine every night — and Toad needed a stove for his pancakes.

'Don't worry,' said Hyena. 'If that's all we need, let me take care of it. By tonight I'll have everything ready.'

Don't ask where they came from: the elegant chairs and tables draped with linen, nor how Hyena got his hands on a stove and Chinese lanterns. Suspended from the bridge on strong cords Spider had spun especially, they bathed everything in warm light.

Bat had been busy, darting around the neighbourhood, distributing invitations.

'I hope you've made enough pancakes, Toadie.' Rat was anxious, but they all felt flustered as they waited for their customers.

'How much longer?' said Toad, looking from his pocket watch to the mountain of pancakes. It was well past midnight and not a single customer had appeared.

Even Hyena, usually so mellow, seemed uncertain, and little by little a familiar gloom settled over the party.

The animals began to blame themselves.

Bat was convinced that horror was all he had managed to spread around the neighbourhood, despite his friendly flitting.

Squatting amidst the pancakes, Toad felt unappetising all over again. Rat stared mutely ahead, and Spider had a bitter taste in her mouth.

'I can't stand it!' Hyena bellowed into the awful silence. 'Toad, serve us a round of pancakes, and let's get started!' He produced his saxophone and the others began to perk up, too.

'Well, why not?' said Rat, taking out his ukulele. 'We have music, we have pancakes, we have one another.'

No one could argue with that. And sure enough, with a hot pancake inside you, the world looks like a different place.

Spider stopped crying, Bat smiled again, Hyena improvised on the sax, and Rat picked his way after him.

The five of them made such a happy racket, it could be heard in the farthest corner of the neighbourhood.

'Something's going on over there!' said Fox to Goose, forgetting he was about to eat her.

'Phew, let's go and have a look,' Goose said quickly.

And so they all turned up: Hare, Hedgehog and Hen, Cow, Cat and Dog, Rabbit, Raven, Pig, Pelican, Monkey and Mole. It turned out to be a wonderful night.

'**W**hat an entrancing party that was,' said the charming chook.

'I should say so,' said Hare, who had had a splendid time. 'Will you be doing it again some time soon?'

Rat looked around at the others. 'From now on, every night until daybreak.' The five fine friends laughed happily together.

This edition first published in Australia and New Zealand 2009
Gecko Press, PO Box 9335, Marion Square, Wellington 6141, New Zealand
Email: info@geckopress.com

National Library of New Zealand Cataloguing-in-Publication Data

Erlbruch, Wolf.
Fürchterlichen Fünf. English
The fearsome five / Wolf Erlbruch.
ISBN 978-1-877467-23-3 — ISBN 978-1-877467-22-6 (pbk.)
[1. Social acceptance—Fiction.] I. Title.
833.914—dc 22

Translated by Catherine Chidgey
Edited by Penelope Todd
Typesetting by Archetype, New Zealand
Printed by Everbest, China

ISBN Hardback: 978-1-877467-23-3
ISBN Paperback: 978-1-877467-22-6

For more curiously good books, visit www.geckopress.com